41540198

D0427112

EL NIÑO!
AND LA NIÑA

THE
WEATHER
CHANNEL®

EL NIÑO!
AND LA NIÑA

by Sally Rose

SIMON SPOTLIGHT

ACKNOWLEDGMENTS
The publisher is grateful to the following individuals for
permission to reproduce their photographs and drawings:

Cover: Michael Bath, Robert Epplett
Insert: Robert Epplett, Lou Sloat

Special thanks to the following for permission to use the first-hand accounts
found in Chapter Six: Jordan Scudder and Nathan Beckett. And special thanks
to William Kessler, NOAA/Pacific Marine Environmental Laboratory; Lou
Sloat, Texas Forest Service; Jo Schwiekhard Moss, Texas State Division of
Emergency Management; and Robert Epplet, California State Office of
Emergency Services.

SIMON SPOTLIGHT
An imprint of Simon & Schuster Children's Publishing Division
1230 Avenue of the Americas, New York, New York 10020

Rose, Sally.
El Niño, La Niña / by Sally Rose.
p. cm.
Includes index.
Summary: Identifies the causes of the phenomena known as El Niño and La Niña,
the differences between them, and why each causes such weather extremes.
ISBN 0-689-82015-1 (pbk.)
1. El Niño Current—Juvenile literature. 2. La Niña Current—Juvenile literature. 3.
Climatic changes—Juvenile literature. I. Title.
GC296.8.E58R68 1999
99-31149   CIP

CONTENTS

1

The Power of El Niño

In the winter of 1997-98, storm after storm pounds the West Coast. On Friday, February 6th, high tides and huge waves clobber California's Santa Cruz coastline, causing damage in some places not equaled since the winter of 1982-83, another El Niño winter. Waves crashing into the waterfront bring driftwood, sand, seaweed, and seawater into restaurants and shops. Businesses and residents up and down the coast have no power. The week's storms have washed out stretches of the coastal highway. Sixteen buildings have been condemned because of mudslides. Mudslides have also blocked off many main roads and washed houses down hillsides.

Several communities have been cut off from the rest of the world. Just south of Santa Cruz, the postmaster must use an Air National Guard helicopter in order to deliver mail from Monterey to Big Sur

Summer 1998: Florida's ablaze. The underbrush in forests across the state has become dry and crackly since the showers and thunderstorms that typically arrive in May were delayed and did not make an appearance until July. Wildfires have been raging across northern Florida since the end of May, leaving large black scars of destruction in their paths. On July 3rd, 45,000 people in Flagler County, Florida, rush to gather whatever belongings they can before evacuating their homes and neighborhoods.

Firefighters have worked round the clock

across four counties to bring the rampaging fires under control. The ground is scorched and dry. One newspaper account in the *St. Petersburg Times* describes the footsteps of evacuated residents returning to their homes across the burned grass as sounding "like crushing potato chips."

What in the world could be influencing these bizarre extremes of weather? You guessed it—El Niño.

Blame It on El Niño

Although El Niño is usually associated with strange weather events, it has been blamed for everything from forest fires burning out of control in Indonesia, to outbreaks of diseases such as malaria and cholera in Peru, to escalating ice cream prices in California. And, truth be known, weather scientists say, El Niño is in part responsible for odd occurrences all over the world. In 1982 the first typhoon in seventy-five years hit French Polynesia. In May 1998 in Neskowin, Oregon, **erosion** from storms uncovered what scientists believe are layers of ancient soil complete with pieces of dead grass. In February 1998, in the Sechura Desert in coastal Peru, runoff from flooding rains created a lake ninety miles long, twenty miles wide, and ten feet deep. The Sechura is usually one of the driest places on Earth. But this lake appears periodically over the centuries and usually dries up after about two years. Although it is not accurate to solely blame El Niño for specific weather occurrences, scientists believe that El Niño, along with other factors, can significantly affect global weather patterns.

Climate Event of the Century

The El Niño of 1997-98 is being referred to as "the climate event of the century." At first no one thought it would surpass the El

Did You Know?

El Niño has even affected the price of ice cream. The 1997-98 El Niño dumped so much rain in California, where one-fifth of the country's milk is produced, that "cows were up to their udders in mud," said one food analyst. Feed quality was down, and when cows don't eat well there is less fat in their milk. This fat, or butterfat, is used to make ice cream. But with less fatty milk, it takes more milk to make enough butterfat for ice cream. So, the cost of butterfat and ice cream went up. Actually, because of the rains, the cost of most dairy products, like butter and cream, rose, too.

Niño of 1982-83, previously considered the biggie of the century. But 1997-98 left the El Niño of 1982-83 in the dust, so to speak.

What Is El Niño?

Basically, El Niño is a warming of the water in the eastern and central equatorial Pacific Ocean. This warming can have effects all over the world. Depending on how warm the water gets, these effects can have devastating consequences. El Niño can cause **drought** in one part of the world and bring flooding rains to other regions of the Earth.

What Is La Niña?

La Niña occurs when the same area of the Pacific Ocean cools from its average temperature. This type of cold event in the Pacific can bring dry, warmer-than-average weather to the southern U.S. and colder-than-average temperatures to the north during the winter. These are the exact opposite effects of El Niño, which usually brings a warm winter to the northern U.S. and lots of rain to the southern U.S.

What's in a Name?

South American fishermen have known for hundreds of years that the waters where they fished, off the coast of Peru and

Ecuador, became slightly warmer for a period of time each year. They also noticed that sometimes, every few years, around the end of December and January, the water would warm up dramatically. During a major warm-up, the fish they sought all but disappeared. In fact, it was these fishermen who named the warming of the waters "El Niño de Navidad," or "the Christ child," because it occurs near Christmastime. Scientists studying the phenomenon then shortened it to "El Niño," which means "the boy" in Spanish. "La Niña" means "the girl."

Effects Felt Far Afield

What the fishermen did not know, however, and what scientists have been discovering since, is that the warming of the waters in the central and eastern equatorial Pacific doesn't have just local impacts. Rather, that warming actually can effect the weather thousands of miles away.

Imagine, if you threw a stone in Dewitt, Illinois, and it broke a window in Cairo, Egypt, more than 6,000 miles away. Pretty neat feat, right? Well, El Niño has a powerful arm, too. Even though it is a phenomenon which occurs in the tropical Pacific Ocean along the equator, it can influence weather all across the globe—from California and Florida, to Indonesia, Australia, southeast Asia, and even Africa.

Some years El Niño is not all that strong. Other years, such as in 1982-83 and 1997-98, it flexes its muscles and makes itself felt around the world, sometimes with devastating results.

2

Where Does El Niño Come From

Puddle in an Ocean

El Niño can be thought of as a giant puddle of warm water along the **equator** in the central and eastern Pacific Ocean. But how does it get there? And why? Scientists are working hard to find out what triggers an El Niño or La Niña. They don't yet know exactly what the causes are, but even as you're reading this, they're learning more and more. The strong El Niño in 1997-98 was a lucky break for weather researchers. The Pacific Ocean became a laboratory for them. And they were able to discover many fascinating new facts about El Niño.

Business as Usual

In order to understand what happens during an El Niño year, it's important to understand what **meteorologists,** or weather scientists, consider "neutral" conditions.

The sun is very strong and very warm in the tropical Pacific. The strong sunlight warms the surface waters along the equator. Winds, called **trade winds,** blow from the northeast north of the equator and from the southeast south of the equator. The trade winds come together near the equator and travel west, parallel to the equator.

The Trade Winds

The sun and wind work together to drive surface ocean currents. The trade winds, blowing east to west across the equatorial waters in the eastern Pacific, push warm surface water toward the west. So warm water tends to pile up at the western end of the Pacific. Where the warm surface water has been dragged away, cooler water from below rises to the surface. As it rises, the cooler water from the ocean deep carries up with it tiny nutrients released from decaying plants and animals on the ocean bed. This process is called **upwelling**. Fish and other sea life in the surface waters depend on these nutrients to live. In fact, most of the fish in the ocean live in the surface waters. So these nutrients are very important.

A Little Pressure Helps

There is an intimate but complex inter-action between the ocean and the **atmosphere**. The warm sea surface in the western part of the tropical Pacific near New Guinea, heats up the air above the ocean, causing it to expand and rise. Expanding, rising air results in **low surface air pressure** over that region. On the other hand, the cooler sea surface toward the

Did You Know?

The trade winds got their name because they blow so regularly, and their pathway along the equator became a popular ship-trading route. For hundreds of years, before there were steamships, sailing ships, which carried cargo to other lands, could depend on trade winds to fill their sails and transport the ships across the oceans.

eastern Pacific keeps the air above the water cool. Cool air is denser and tends to sink, causing **high air pressure** at the surface. Along the equator, air blows from high pressure toward low pressure, which means from east to west. This process reinforces the usual trade winds, blowing from east to west.

Which Came First, the Chicken or the Egg?

Billy Kessler, an oceanographer at the National Oceanographic and Atmospheric Administration (NOAA), studies El Niño from the Pacific Marine Environmental Laboratory in Seattle. He describes this ocean-atmosphere interaction in the tropical Pacific as "a chicken and egg situation." He explains: "If you ask me 'Why are there trade winds?' I will say 'That's simple, there are trade winds because the water is cold in the east and warm in the west.' But if you ask me 'Why is the water cold in the east and warm in the west?' I'll say 'That's simple, too. It's because there are trade winds.'" In other words, the winds determine the water temperature but the water temperature also determines the winds. The actions of the ocean and the atmosphere are so intertwined it is difficult to tell which comes first and what causes what.

El Niño Changes Everything

During an El Niño, everything changes. In fact, everything goes in reverse. On a very basic level the El Niño story goes like this: The trade winds heading west in the equatorial Pacific begin to weaken, and can eventually reverse. As the trade winds weaken, they don't drag as much surface water west. The usual upwelling of the cooler, subsurface water near South America lessens and may even stop, causing the surface water in the eastern equatorial Pacific to warm, which further weakens the trade winds. Also, not as many nutrients reach the ocean surface across this region. Weather satellites from NOAA have revealed dramatic warming across the eastern and central tropical Pacific. Air tends to rise above the relatively warm water. The rising air warms and moistens the atmosphere, and it disrupts the usual path of the **jet streams**. Jet streams are narrow, fast-moving currents of air in the upper atmosphere that influence weather patterns. The disruption in the usual path of the jet streams can cause changes to weather all around the globe.

Harsh Force

Some of El Niño's harshest impacts occur near the equator. The deserts along the narrow coastal strip in Peru get heavy rainfall and flooding. Indonesia suffers drought.

Some scientists believe El Niño may be responsible in part for the warming of ocean water west of Central America and off the west coast of the U.S. Fish in these normally rich waters have less food and many die off. And the birds, mammals, and fishermen who rely on those fish suffer, too. This ocean warming is also one factor that can allow eastern Pacific hurricanes to grow stronger. Although scientists don't yet know what triggers an El Niño event, they are learning a lot about what goes on during one.

El Niño's Mirror Image—La Niña

La Niña is the name given to what is called a "cold event" in the eastern equatorial Pacific. During a La Niña, the waters off the northwestern coast of South America become colder than average. They may cool about four degrees Fahrenheit. During an El Niño, on the other hand, the waters can heat up by as much as fifteen degrees. La Niña does not appear to occur as often as El Niño. And it often brings the opposite effects as El Niño to parts of the world. For example, across the southern U.S., where El Niño winters tend to be wet, La Niña winters are typically drier and warmer than average.

El Niño-Southern Oscillation

El Niño and La Niña refer only to the temperature of the ocean in the tropical Pacific. As discussed earlier, the ocean temperature affects the surface air pressure and winds across that part of the world. During an El Niño, the air pressure over Tahiti becomes unusually low, and the air pressure over Darwin, Australia, is unusually high. During a La Niña, it is just the opposite. Changes to air pressure across the tropical Pacific are called the Southern

Oscillation. To **oscillate** means to swing back and forth, like a pendulum. Scientists don't completely understand what triggers the combined oceanic-atmospheric system named **El Niño-Southern Oscillation,** or ENSO.

What's So Unusual?

El Niño and La Niña events are often referred to as "atypical," "unusual," "abnormal,"—all words meaning different from the usual. But in reality, El Niño and La Niña are typical occurrences. They are simply extremes in the natural variation of equatorial Pacific ocean temperatures. An El Niño event usually lasts about a year, and it is part of a cycle that seems to occur every two to five years on average. La Niñas typically occur a bit less frequently than El Niño.

3

Extreme Weather

Floods, droughts, ice storms! El Niño and La Niña can influence all kinds of severe weather. A strong El Niño can bring torrential rains and floods to usually dry lands, and can create lakes in what is normally a desert. On the flip side, El Niño can also cause unusually dry conditions in rain forest regions, bringing the danger of destructive forest fires. El Niño's effects can reach as far north as Canada and as far south as New Zealand, and east to west all around the globe.

Fire! Flood! Drought! Tornado!

Could all these phenomena be influenced by El Niño? Just because the water temperature in parts of the Pacific Ocean is a few degrees warmer than average? Well, yes. It seems El Niño's bag of tricks is large and varied. In the 1982-83 El Niño made worse the already devastating drought in Africa, and had a hand in the worst drought in 200 years in Australia. It was also linked to droughts in Hawaii, Mexico, the Philippines, and Indonesia. But in Peru and Ecuador it brought torrential rains and flooding. Intense winter storms clobbered the West Coast of the United States, while Louisiana and Florida were hit with floods.

El Niño Slows Earth!
During the 1997-98 El Niño, scientists at NASA discovered that El Niño-related winds actually caused the Earth's rotation to slow. This slowing made the days longer than normal, but only by milliseconds. February 5, 1998 was the longest of the longer-than-usual days—the extra-strong winds added 0.6 milliseconds onto that day (that's less than one-thousandth of a second)!

French Polynesia usually goes years and years between **typhoons,** but the El Niño of 1982-83 ushered in seven. One of those left 25,000 people homeless on Tahiti. A series of El Niño events that occurred from 1991 to 1995 played a role in launching a wave of record-breaking weather oddities worldwide. A whole year's worth of rain and snow fell in California in January of 1995. Germany, Holland, Belgium, and France experienced their worst flooding in a century. And drought dried up Australia, Indonesia, and southern Africa.

El Niño Takes on California

California's weather goes to extremes thanks to El Niño. When an El Niño occurs, it makes itself felt throughout the large state. And it's not always in the same way. During a 1976-77 El Niño, Northern California suffered a record drought. In contrast, during the 1982-83 El Niño, rainstorms did millions of dollars in damage up and down California's coast. The El Niños of 1992-93 and 1994-95, too, brought heavy rainfall to California. In the winter of 1998, on February 6th, a chain of storms struck up and down the length of the state. Snowstorms blasted the northern part of the state in the Sierra Nevada mountains. In Glenn County, north of Sacramento, several of the major highways were closed because of blizzard conditions.

Although El Niño can help bring flooding rains to California, the state sometimes experiences devastating rains during non-El Niño years, too.

4

El Niño Talks to the Animals

Although we see and read more about its effect on people and buildings, El Niño causes a variety of conditions that have an extreme effect on animals of all kinds. From tiny algae, to huge marine mammals, El Niño disrupts their lives by changing the environment in their usual feeding grounds.

Up from the Deep

Just like animals on land, animals in the sea need sunlight to live. Therefore, most marine life exists in the upper surface waters where sunlight can penetrate. In the eastern equatorial Pacific, animals living in the surface waters depend on the process of upwelling. When warm surface water is pushed out of the way by winds, cold water from below moves up to take its place. That cold water, brought up by upwelling, carries lots of nutrients. Tiny microscopic plants, called **phytoplankton**, and tiny animals called **zooplankton**, eat these nutrients from the deep. The plankton are in turn eaten by fish and other marine animals. Part of what triggers an El Niño is that upwelling slows down or stops in this area of the eastern Pacific, near Peru. When upwelling decreases, fewer nutrients are brought to the surface of the ocean, which means there is less food for the marine life. Some of the fish die and some leave this warm area of the Pacific in search of food.

There's No Place Like the Galapagos

The Galapagos Islands are home to a variety of fascinating animals—marine iguanas, Darwin's finches, sea lions, Galapagos penguins, flightless cormorants, and more. During an El Niño, the waters around these islands can warm significantly. In May, University of Washington zoologist Dee Boersma traveled to the Galapagos to study how the 1997-98 El Niño affected animal life there. One of the animals Boersma studied was the Galapagos penguin. She found many fewer penguins than normal, and they looked skinny and underfed. And, she could find no penguin chicks anywhere. To feed, the

A flood brought on by massive rains created this scene in Comal County, Texas. In October, 1998, floods covered three dozen counties in south central Texas, an area the size of Arkansas.

Like Texas, California often gets hit hard during El Niño winters. The sign above sums up the obvious in these scenes of flooded-out neighborhoods caused by heavy rains in Northern California.

In October of 1995, Hurricane Opal made landfall on the panhandle of Florida and caused much destruction to these homes in Pensacola.

s flood waters retreat, they often leave in their wake a
ebris-strewn trail of destruction, like at this farmhouse
ear the American River in Northern California.

Above, a Texas Forest Service firefighter battles the Cibola Creek Fire, which burned nearly 63,000 acres near Marfa, Texas. Below, lightning started this 14,000 acre fire in the Matador Wildlife Management Area.

By spring of 1998, parts of Texas were experiencing their worst drought since the early 1900s. The weather pattern at that time was likely influenced by the lingering El Niño that had begun during the previous spring. More than 12,000 wildfires burned more than half a million acres.

This wildfire in East Texas is "crowning out," which means it is burning through the tops of the trees.

Tornadoes that struck on April 25, 1994 damaged many homes and other buildings in Lancaster, Texas, near Dallas.

two-foot tall, flightless birds dive off the rocky shores of the island into the water to hunt for medium-sized fish called mullet. But because of the strong El Niño, few mullet could be found in the surrounding waters. Boersma guessed that, because of the lack of fish for food, either none of the penguins bred in the last six months or none of the chicks survived, or a combination of both.

Coral Reefs

Another victim of the warm waters of El Niño is coral reefs. Coral reefs are fragile **ecosystems** where many types of plants and animals live. Coral is an animal that secretes a limestone skeleton. The basic structure for a reef is made up by this limestone. Many individual corals make up a reef. Lots of other sea animals feed in and around the coral. Algae called zooxanthallae live within the coral. The zooxanthallae

Famous evolutionist Charles Darwin, who lived from 1808 to 1882, based his theories of evolution on his studies of Galapagos finches. Some scientists now believe that El Niño may be a strong, determining force in the evolution of species, especially those living in the Galapagos.

give off oxygen and nutrients that the coral needs to survive. The algae also give the coral pigmentation, or color. When the ocean waters warm up to temperatures the corals aren't used to, as during an El Niño, it can cause the corals to "spit out" their tiny zooxanthallae guests. Without the algae, the coral loses its coloring. This process is called "bleaching." If warm temperatures last too long around the reef area, the coral doesn't get its usual supply of nutrients and may die. If the coral dies, the rest of the plants and animals living on the reef could die as well. The 1982-83 El Niño played havoc with coral reefs around

Costa Rica, Panama, Colombia, and the Galapagos Islands. Seventy to ninety-five percent of the corals in those areas died that year from the overheated waters.

During the first six months of 1998, bleaching occurred in the coral reefs in areas around Malaysia, Indonesia, Seychelles, Kenya, Somalia, Madagascar, Sri Lanka, India, and Cambodia, among others.

Seals and Sea Lions

Because seals and sea lions live on squid, anchovy, sardine, rockfish, and herring, among others, they, too, are affected by El Niño. For the past twenty-five years, scientists have been studying seals and sea lions on San Miguel Island, part of a chain of islands called the Channel Islands off the California coast. They found that during the El Niños of 1972-73, 1982-83, 1991-92, and 1997-98, the seals and sea lions had many fewer pups than usual. Also, their pups did not grow as fast, and many did not survive. In 1983 northern fur seals gave birth to fewer than half the usual number of pups than the year before. And further study tracking those few pups found that none appeared to survive. California sea lion births went down by thirty to seventy percent on all of the Channel Islands. During the 1991-92 El Niño, two out of every three pups died in their first year.

The Insects of El Niño

Ants, ticks, millipedes, centipedes, earwigs, termites, killer bees, mosquitoes, ladybird beetles, aphids, and grasshoppers are just a few of the pesky type critters that often get a boost from El Niño. Because the winter of 1997-98 was so warm and wet in many places in the United States, thanks to

El Niño can mean plenty of food for animals that live in the forest. A warm, wet winter and spring encourages lush plant growth, which means plenty of leaves, seeds, and nuts for forest creatures to eat. With plenty of food, the plant-eating animals such as insects, birds, rodents, and deer, grow strong and can produce many young. In turn, they are then food for other, larger animals. Of course, in areas where El Niño's influence helps to bring on a drought, the effects can be just the opposite.

El Niño, many insect eggs laid the previous spring and summer survived. And when they hatched, they found plenty of plants to feed on that had also grown up bushy and tall from the rainy, early spring.

On the East Coast, especially in southern New England, millions of mosquito eggs survived the warm winter. By spring they were buzzing everywhere. Because of all the rain during spring, those mosquitoes then found abundant pools of standing water where they, in turn, could lay eggs upon eggs upon eggs. In a similar occurrence in April of 1998, Southern California experienced "The Invasion of the Grasshoppers." Grasshoppers swarmed the streets and parking lots of the Southwest and Southern California, even causing the evacuation of a jury room at a courthouse in Indio, California.

5

Studying El Niño

Scientists have been studying the El Niño-Southern Oscillation phenomenon only since the El Niño of 1972-73. So it is a relatively new field of study. In studying El Niño, scientists look at a variety of things: 1) how changes in the ocean, like currents and upwelling, cause sea surface temperatures to rise; 2) how the warming of the sea surface brings about changes in the atmosphere and clouds; 3) how changes in the atmosphere affect surface winds; and

4) how changes in winds affect the sea surface temperature.

Scientists are studying these effects in order to try and predict when an El Niño or La Niña might occur. Some scientists think El Niños are occurring more frequently now than in recent history.

Forecasting

What good would it do to know when an El Niño year might occur? Researchers believe that forecasting an El Niño event up to a year in advance could help save tremendous amounts of money for businesses, especially those related to fishing and farming. And cities and towns might be able to prepare for flooding rains by clearing canals or building up barriers around creeks and rivers. Or, in areas where ENSO brings months of dry weather and drought, cities and towns could prepare by saving and rationing water beforehand.

Technology Uncovers Clues to El Niño

Scientists use all sorts of equipment to study El Niño—satellites, ocean buoys, airplanes, lasers, and computers. The Pacific Marine Environmental Laboratory in Seattle, where oceanographer Billy Kessler works, developed and maintains the Tropical Atmosphere Ocean (TAO) buoy array. Approximately 300 buoys are moored at seventy locations across the equatorial Pacific. These buoys measure sea surface temperatures, sub-surface temperatures, surface winds, air temperature, and humidity. "Together all the buoys constitute a huge instrument, and it lets us see things we never saw before," says Kessler. The buoys beam up information to

Did You Know?

Scientists also use a variety of high-tech instruments to study the effects of El Niño and La Niña. Researchers at NOAA, NASA, and U.S. Geological Survey are using lasers mounted on planes to study El Niño's impact on West Coast beaches and coastal cliffs. The planes fly back and forth along the coast while the lasers scan overlapping 1,000-foot strips of the coastline. Scientists will use the scans to make maps of the coast prior to an El Niño winter season, and then again several months later. The maps will show how much erosion took place. They plan to use the information to predict the effects of coastal storms and to help communities better plan building development.

satellites, which in turn send the data back down to Earth to be used by forecasters and scientists. Satellites also help the research effort by sending photos of the ocean and atmosphere back to Earth, such as those that helped to track the warm pool of El Niño in the Pacific. Computers are also used to make models of possible weather scenarios to aid in predictions.

Farmers and Fisherman

Knowing that an El Niño or La Niña is going to occur could be very helpful for many people, especially farmers. Not only could farmers adjust which fields they plant in, they could plant crops that they know have a better chance of withstanding different types of severe weather. Thanks to the discoveries of scientists, when strawberry farmers in California heard predictions of an El Niño in 1997, they decided to prepare. They planted their crops in higher, well-drained fields. It paid off. The lowland fields where they usually plant were flooded during that year's strong El Niño.

Nature's Clues

In order to study El Niño and La Niña, researchers use a lot of high-tech equipment. But they also rely on lower tech tools, such as those they find in nature. For example, scientists called **dendrochronologists** study growth rings in tree trunks to try and figure out if the frequency of El Niños is on the rise. Coral reefs, too, offer clues. Just like trees, each year as they grow, coral reefs leave layers of limestone skeleton. During a year when the coral has a lot of growth, a thick layer is visible. If there was little growth, the layer is thinner. When the water temperature is too warm, or too cold, the coral grows less. Scientists can use these layers to look back in history and tell when El Niño and La Niña events might have occurred. Scientists studying coral near the Dominican Republic discovered a history of El Niño s dating all the way back 5,000 years ago.

6

Harsh Force:
People Affected by El Niño

El Niños typically occur every two to five years, so there have been a lot of them throughout history. But scientists have only been studying them for a short time. Unfortunately, not much information is available about most of the El Niños and La Niñas that occurred before 1982-83. But scientists have figured out when past El Niños and La Niñas have occurred, and which appear to have been particularly strong.

A Time line of Destruction

The Earth Space Research Group at the University of California at Santa Barbara made a list of events that occurred during the 1982-83 El Niño. Here are some of the high points:

JUNE 1982

•West-going trade winds along equatorial Pacific Ocean reverse direction
•Warm water pool in western Pacific starts moving eastward along the equator
•Dry spell begins in Australia, Indonesia and New Guinea

SEPTEMBER 1982

•Sea surface temperatures are five degrees Celsius higher than normal
•The usual abundance of marine wildlife disappears

November 1982

•French Polynesia is devastated by the first of seven major tropical cyclones

June 1983

•Deserts of Peru, Ecuador and Bolivia receive 146 inches of rain, instead of five inches
•Galapagos Islands receive more rain in six weeks than in six average years
•Driest summer on record in Pacific part of Australia results in huge brush fires and crop and livestock losses
•Nineteen African countries endure severe droughts
•California and the Rockies suffer $1.1 billion damage from rains and floods

El Niño of 1997-98

Most weather scientists agree, the El

Niño of 1997-98 was one of the strongest climatic events in recorded history. NOAA researcher Billy Kessler thinks the most amazing aspects of the 1997-98 El Niño were: 1)The extreme rainfall—almost thirty-nine inches of rain fell in the eastern-central Pacific during the month of December, a region where the typical rainfall is about 11.7 inches a year; and 2)The highest sea surface temperature ever measured in the eastern Pacific occurred in that El Niño year.

Living Through It

People all over the world were affected by the variety of weather conditions influenced by El Niño and La Niña. Here are a few personal accounts of kids who had close encounters.

Jordan, from Florida, helped put out small fires in his neighborhood, which was devastated by the wildfires of 1998. Here's what he remembers about that experience.

Jordan's Story

On Thursday about eleven o'clock in the morning, the firemen came telling everyone on our street they had thirty minutes to get out, because the fire was half a mile away. There were about seventeen houses that completely burned down, and most of the other houses had some kind of damage. People lost furniture, clothes, pictures, and everything else they owned. When we were driving away from our house, the sky was all black and it looked like it was snowing, but it was just ashes. After being evacuated for five days we were told we could go home. As we drove back into Matanzas Woods, it was so different, there were no woods left. Everything was black. So many houses were burned to the ground. That night as my family and I were looking around our house in the woods, we saw all kinds of little fires. We got out buckets and pails and filled them with water from our swimming pool and started putting the fires out. I was happy that the firemen saved my house. I know that they did the best job that they could do. And I wish this would not happen again to anyone else, because it was scary.

—Jordan Scudder, age ten

Nathan and Elias Beckett, with their seven-year-old brother Caleb, helped to protect their church when La Honda Creek, in Northern California, flooded over during one of the drenching storms that arrived with the El Niño of 1997-98. Here's what Nathan remembers:

Nathan's Story

On January 6th, it started to rain late in the afternoon and by the time my brothers and I went to bed it was raining like the clouds had picked up the ocean and dumped it on us! I woke up in the morning to find my dad gone to help evacuate stuff from the cottage at our local church. The cottage was situated on the banks of the now raging creek. The creek had risen until it had overflowed it's banks and covered the cabin floor with mud two or three feet thick! We then drove around town and saw collapsed and washed-out roads. A lot of people had to evacuate their homes because their own were sliding away or falling down. Six houses in my town slid and their owners had to abandon them. Later we found out that we had gotten four inches of rain in two hours. At that time we did not know that El Niño had reached all the way down to South America, but now I know that what we had happen here was nothing compared to what happened down there.

—Nathan Beckett, age twelve

7

Safety: Be Prepared!

Disasters can occur anywhere and at any time. Staying safe and being prepared before severe weather occurs is very important. Here are some simple suggestions to follow that will help you and your family be prepared for whatever weather El Niño or La Niña might send your way.

Disaster Plan and Supplies

Make a disaster plan with your family.

Discuss what each member of the family will do to prepare for the severe weather, and what you will do if it strikes. It's very important to keep a disaster kit easily accessible. Your kit should contain at least three days worth of food. Ready-to-eat food and food that doesn't need to be kept in the refrigerator is best. Here's some suggestions of what to keep in your disaster kit:

- Battery-operated radio
- Flashlight
- Extra batteries
- Water
- Food and vitamins
- First aid kit (one for your home and one for each car)
- Prescription and nonprescription medicines
- Tools and supplies (paper cups, utility knife, hammer, matches, etc.)
- Cleaning supplies
- Clothing and bedding
- Special necessities for babies or senior citizens

- Important family documents
- Entertainment (games and books)

If you live in an area that might experience floods, drought, hurricanes, tornadoes, or wildfires, here are some suggestions for how to be prepared and stay safe.

FLOODS:

1. Because basements are usually below ground, they can easily flood. Keep your valuables and electrical appliances out of the basement.

2. Tell your parents to make sure all utility meters and the main breaker or fuse box for your house are above the flood level in your area.

HURRICANES AND TORNADOES:

1. Make sure you have hurricane straps holding your roof to your walls.

2. Protect your windows with storm shut-

ters or plywood when severe weather is approaching.

DROUGHT:

1. Conserve water:
   a. Don't leave faucets dripping.
   b. Install water-saving devices in your showers and toilets.

TO HELP PREVENT FIRES:

1. Clear away dead brush from your yard.
2. Cut dead or dying wood from the trees and bushes around your house.

Web Sites

The Weather Channel and Red Cross have teamed up to create the national safety and preparedness initiative called Project Safeside: Keeping You Ahead of the Storm. These two sites, one sponsored by

The Weather Channel and the other by the Red Cross, have important safety tips for how to prepare for severe weather and what to do when it hits. Both have colorful graphics and photos.

http://www.weather.com/safeside/
or http://www.redcross.org/safeside/

The Federal Emergency Management Agency (FEMA) has put together this Web site for kids. FEMA for Kids has colorful, humorous icons that lead to all sorts of helpful, kid-friendly information including one on El Niño.

http://www.fema.gov/kids/

Glossary

ATMOSPHERE—The layers of air that surround the Earth.

COLD FRONT—The leading edge of a moving mass of cold air.

DENDROCHRONOLOGIST—A scientist who studies tree growth rings to find out, among other things, how old a tree is.

DROUGHT—A long period during which a region has below average rainfall.

ECOSYSTEM—A community of plants and animals that influence each other and work as a unit in nature.

EL NIÑO-SOUTHERN OSCILLATION (ENSO)—Interactions between the ocean and the atmosphere that include the warming of the water in the eastern and central equatorial Pacific and the changes in surface air pressure due to that warming. ENSO can disrupt the usual path of jet streams, which in turn can cause radical changes to the Earth's weather patterns.

EQUATOR—The ideal or conceptual circle around the Earth that divides the planet into northern and southern hemispheres.

EROSION—The action of water or wind wearing away rock, sand or soil.

FLASH FLOOD—A localized flood caused by very heavy rain falling in a short period of time.

HIGH SURFACE AIR PRESSURE—Cold ocean water tends to cool the air above it. Cool air is dense and tends to sink. The sinking air causes high surface air pressure.

JET STREAM—Jet streams are fast-moving

currents of air in the upper atmosphere that influence weather patterns.

LOW SURFACE AIR PRESSURE—When the air above the ocean's surface is heated by warm water, the air begins to expand and rise. Expanding, rising air causes low surface air pressure.

METEOROLOGIST—A scientist who studies weather. By looking at what is happening in the atmosphere, meteorologists predict the weather.

OSCILLATE—To swing back and forth, like a pendulum.

PHYTOPLANKTON—Tiny plants that drift around in ocean waters.

TRADE WINDS—Winds that blow from the northeast north of the equator and from the southeast south of the equator.

Usually, the trade winds come together near the equator and travel west, parallel to the equator. During an El Niño, the trade winds weaken and can even reverse direction.

TYPHOON—A tropical cyclone with the maximum sustained surface winds of seventy-four miles per hour or higher that occurs in the western Pacific Ocean.

UPWELLING—When warmer surface water is dragged away by wind, cool nutrient-rich water from below rises to the surface.

ZOOPLANKTON—Tiny animals that drift around in ocean waters.

Index